The Mystery TRAIL

Are you ready for a story,
Poppy Cat...?

One day, Poppy Cat and her **friends** were playing in the garden when Mo arrived with a brilliant **detective** kit. It was **full** of fantastic disguises! "I'd love to be a detective looking for clues!" said Poppy Cat.

"I'm **ready**," said Alma. "All we need is a mystery to solve . . ."

Just then, Owl arrived all in a **flap**. "**Help!** One of my books has **gone** missing!" he cried.

"Help!"

"PERFECT!" said Poppy Cat.
"Now we've got a **real**
mystery to solve.
Come on, let's return to the
scene of the **crime!**"

Everyone **piled** into Owl's tree house and **busily** hunted for **clues**.

"Aha!
Found one!"

cried Alma.

"And I've
found one **too**,"

said Zuzu.

Poppy Cat held the **clues** up for a **closer** look. "Hmm," she said, "I have **no idea** where that blue **feather** has come from."

"But this purple pine cone must come from the **Purple Pine Forest!**"

"Can we go there **right** away?" Owl asked.

"Of course!" said Poppy Cat. "But first we're going to need . . . our very own car!"

And off they sped.

Soon the friends **reached** the **Purple** **Pine** Forest.

Mo spotted another **purple** pine cone. Poppy Cat **held** it up.

"Hmm, **not** as purple as the one we found in **Owl's** house ... which means it's the **right** forest, but the **WRONG** tree!"

They searched **deeper** in the forest . . .

"**Nothing here!**" called **Zuzu**.

Then they found their friend **Egbert**, dressed up as

Ernie the **Tree-hugging** Tortoise.

So Poppy Cat joined in!

e was **busy** giving every tree a **hug** . . .

Suddenly, they heard a **strange** **squawking** sound. Egbert ran away!

A pine cone **dropped** **down** from a **nearby** tree!

Owl **spotted** another feather!

They all went to **look** under the **NEXT** tree . . .

At that moment they **heard** a loud "SHUSH!"

They **peered** up and **THERE** was . . . Gilda!

"**Quiet please!**"

she twittered.
This is the Purple Pine Forest
Library Tree and there's
no talking allowed!"

"There's **my** book!"

yelled Owl suddenly, spotting his **long-lost** book.

"This is a **library** book," said Gilda. "You **forgot** to return it, so I **collected** it."

"**Whoops, sorry!**"

said Owl.

"**Thank you Gilda!**"

"Case **solved!**"

said Poppy Cat.

"Nice work detectives!"

and they **all** cheered.

Poppy Cat and the gang stayed on **choosing**

books at the library until

the sun started to **set**.

"We'd better **remember** to bring our **books** back **next** time, though!" chuckled Poppy Cat.

When they arrived **home**, the friends all agreed that being a **detective** was great **fun** and hoped they would do it again soon!

"Bye! Bye!"

"See you soon!"